Zeke Meeks

Zeke Meeks is published by
Picture Window Books
A Capstone Imprint
1710 Roe Crest Drive
North Mankato, MN 56003
www.capstonepub.com

Super cool glasses.

Copyright ©2013 Picture Window Books

Library of Congress Cataloging in Publication Data
Green, D. L. (Debra L.)
  Zeke Meeks vs the no-fun fund-raiser / by D. L. Green; illustrated by Josh Alves.
    p. cm. — (Zeke Meeks)
  Summary: Zeke's school is having a fund-raiser and the student who sell the most cake mix
will get four tickets to Thrillsville Amusement Park, but Zeke is not having much luck until his
great-grandmother gives him a lesson in salesmanship — and he takes his little sister with him.
  ISBN 978-1-4048-7640-8 (library binding)
  1. Money-making projects for children—Juvenile fiction. 2. Selling—Juvenile fiction. 3. Middle-
born children—Juvenile fiction. 4. Brothers and sisters—Juvenile fiction. 5. Great-grandmothers—
Juvenile fiction. 6. Elementary schools—Juvenile fiction. [1. Moneymaking projects—Fiction. 2.
Selling—Fiction. 3. Middle-born children—Fiction. 4. Brothers and sisters—Fiction. 5. Great-
grandmothers—Fiction. 6. Elementary schools—Fiction. 7. Schools—Fiction. 8. Humorous stories.] I.
Alves, Josh. ill. II. Title. III. Title: Zeke Meeks versus the no-fun fund-raiser. IV. Series: Green,
D. L. (Debra L.) Zeke Meeks.
  PZ7.G81926Zgr 2013
  813.6—dc23   2012028194

Vector Credits: Shutterstock
Book design by K. Fraser

Printed in the United States of America
in Stevens Point, Wisconsin.
092012   006937WZS13

This is cake mix.
A lot of it. I sure
hope my neighbors
like cake! Everybody
likes cake, right?

Zeke Meeks
vs THE NO-FUN FUND-RAISER

BY
D. L. GREEN

ILLUSTRATED BY
JOSH ALVES

WARNING: You might get sick of cake before the end of this story.

TABLE OF

CHAPTER 1:

Vomit and Other Things Better Than Math 6

CHAPTER 2:

Sisters Make the WORST Sitters 16

↳ If you have a big sister, you know.

CHAPTER 3:

Worrying Plus More Worrying Equals A LOT of Worrying 32

CHAPTER 4:

Neighbor Labor 42

CHAPTER 5:

Zebe's Cane (Tricks) 54

You gotta see 'em to believe 'em!

BOYS RULE EVERYTHING BUT THE PLAYGROUND

CONTENTS

CHAPTER 6:

Great-Gran's GREAT Ideas 70

CHAPTER 7:

Zeke Meeks vs. Grace Chang's Mom and Dad 82

CHAPTER 8:

FOUR Tickets for SIX People Equals a VERY Hard

Math Problem 92

↳ 4 + 6 = FAIL

CHAPTER 9:

A KILLER Day 104

CHAPTER 10:

My Hero, the Interrupting Principal 112

It may be hard to believe, but it's true!

At least I don't
have to sell
Cane Mist.

NE MIST

GIRLS DROOL ALL BUT GRACE — SHE BITES

Vomit
and Other Things
Better Than
Math

Why is it ALWAYS bugs?!

My teacher, Mr. McNutty, said the three worst words in the universe: "Time for math."

Ugh. I hated math time. There is nothing worse than learning math.

Except for insects. I'm scared of insects. But that's the only thing worse than math.

Also, Grace Chang is worse than math. She's an evil girl in my class with long, sharp, evil fingernails.

But there's nothing else worse than math. Except maybe a gigantic bomb so powerful it would wipe out the entire world. That would be terrible, but at least it would destroy all the math books.

"Turn to page forty-six in your math textbooks," Mr. McNutty said.

I opened my textbook with a frown. Actually, I opened it with my hand. But I had a frown on my face while I did it.

Mr. McNutty said, "Let's explore the metric system of measure —"

He was interrupted by a loud, long bell.

My frown turned into a smile. We were having a fire drill! Hooray! I rushed to the classroom door. Mr. McNutty led everyone outside.

"I hope we get to skip math today," I told my best friend, Hector Cruz.

"I hope it's just a drill and not a real fire," he said.

"Oh, yeah. That too," I said.

A few minutes later, our principal said, "This is just a drill. There's no fire. Everyone please return to class with your teacher."

Mr. McNutty quickly led us back to our classroom. He said, "Let's get started on the math lesson."

I frowned again.

Laurie Schneider raised her hand.

"Please save your questions until after we talk about the assignment," the teacher said.

"But —"

"We have a lot of math to cover," he said.

Then Laurie threw up all over her desk.

Mr. McNutty sighed. "I suppose you were trying to tell me you felt sick."

Laurie nodded.

"I'm sorry," he said.

After Laurie went to the nurse's office and the janitor cleaned up the vomit, Mr. McNutty said, "Finally, let's start the math lesson."

Then the principal's voice came over the loudspeaker. She said,

DON'T FORGET TO GO TO THE AUDITORIUM. THE FUND-RAISING ASSEMBLY STARTS IN TWO MINUTES.

Mr. McNutty asked, "How will I ever get time to teach math?"

I hoped he never would.

We went to the auditorium. A woman stood onstage by a large box. She said, "I'm Mrs. Smedley, the president of the PTA. Do you kids like cake?"

Everyone cheered.

"Wouldn't you love your choice of delicious chocolate, vanilla, or lemon cake?" Mrs. Smedley asked.

Everyone cheered again.

I stared at the big box. I bet it contained three huge cakes for everyone to eat.

"I have something very sweet and very tasty inside this box." Mrs. Smedley pointed to it. "Would you like to see what it is?"

Everyone cheered a third time.

It took Mrs. Smedley a long time to open the box. I licked my lips. I tried to decide what kind of cake to choose. I wondered if I could have a little bit of each.

Mrs. Smedley finally opened the big box. She pulled out three small boxes and held them up.

"These are cake mixes. People who buy them from you can make delicious cakes. And the school gets half the money they spend."

I slumped in my seat. This assembly wasn't much better than a math lesson. I didn't want to sell cake mix or anything else.

Then Mrs. Smedly said, "The student who sells the *most* cake mix will get four tickets to Thrillsville Amusement Park."

I sat up in my seat. I loved Thrillsville! A new ride, Mount Killer, was opening there soon. It was supposed to be very steep and very scary and very cool. It would be amazing to win tickets to Thrillsville for my friends and me.

"I hope you sell a lot of cake mix so you can help our school," Mrs. Smedley said.

I hoped to sell a lot of cake mix so I could help myself.

Sisters Make the WORST Sitters

"How was school?" Mom asked when I got home.

"Boring as usual," I said. "Laurie Schneider threw up on her desk. Also, we had a fire drill and an assembly."

"That doesn't sound boring to me," Mom said. She gave my sister Mia and me a snack of apple slices and peanut butter. She gave our dog, Waggles, a dog bone.

"Waggles looks silly, and not in a good way," I said. He wore pink booties on his paws.

"I think he looks pretty, in a very good way," Mia said. "It took me a long time to get those booties on him."

My older sister, Alexa, smiled and nodded. She was sitting at the table with us, listening to music with headphones.

I decided to test whether she could hear us. I said, "Alexa, is it true that you like licking frogs?"

She smiled and nodded to the music.

Mia giggled.

Then I asked, "Alexa, will you clean my room every day for the next year?"

Alexa kept smiling and nodding.

Mia and I laughed.

"Don't tease your sister," Mom said.

"Okay, Mom. Will you buy cake mix to help my school?" I asked her.

Mom frowned. "Another school fund-raiser? I already gave money for the Jog-A-Thon, made brownies for the bake sale, and bought wrapping paper and magazines. I've spent a lot of money on fund-raisers this year."

Mia said, "That reminds me of a Princess Sing-Along song."

I groaned. Princess Sing-Along was the star of Mia's favorite TV show. It was my *least* favorite TV show.

Mia sang in a screechy voice, "Put some money away, la la la. Save for a rainy day, la la la."

"That song makes no sense. When it rains, people usually stay home. We don't go out shopping in the rain. So we don't need money on rainy days," I said.

"Don't insult Princess Sing-Along." Mia picked up her Princess Sing-Along doll.

"I didn't insult Princess Sing-Along," I said. "If I were to insult her, I'd call her Princess Screech-Along or Princess Sing-Awful or Princess Sing-Atrocious."

"You just insulted her even more. Her feelings are hurt," Mia said.

I shook my head. "Princess Sing-Along can't hear me. Even if she could, she has no feelings to hurt. She's a doll."

"She's a doll with very good hearing and lots of feelings. She's very insulted. You should tell her you're sorry," Mia said.

I stuck out my tongue.

"Kids, please stop arguing. I'll buy a box of cake mix," Mom said.

"How about buying three boxes of cake mix? That way we can try every flavor," I said.

Mom sighed. "All right. I sure spend a lot of money on school fund-raisers. I hope this is the last one."

"I'm sure it is. For this month," I said. "As soon as I finish my snack, will you take me around the neighborhood? I want to sell cake mix to everyone who lives nearby."

"I can't today. I made plans to visit your great-grandmother," Mom said.

Now I sighed. "But what if someone else from my school sells cake mix to the neighbors before I can get to them?"

"I have to keep my promise to see your Great-Gran. She just moved into a nursing home. I need to spend some time with her to help her settle in. Why don't you come with me?" Mom asked. "I know Great-Gran would love to see you."

"I can't. I'm too busy," I lied. Really, I didn't want to go to a nursing home filled with old people. It sounded boring and kind of icky and a little scary.

"Alexa, you need to babysit your brother and sister," Mom said.

Alexa kept smiling and nodding to her music.

Mom took off Alexa's headphones. She told her, "I'm leaving Mia and Zeke home with you. Be a good babysitter. Help them if they need anything."

"No problem. We'll all do our homework," Alexa said.

As soon as Mom left, Alexa turned on the TV.

"What about your homework?" I asked her.

"I'm not going to do homework while Mom's away," she said.

Then she flipped through the TV channels. She stopped at the Special Moments channel and said, "Ooh, *Last, Final Kiss* is on. I love this movie."

I looked at the TV. A pale, pretty woman lay in a hospital bed. Next to her, a guy with huge muscles held her hand. Slow music played in the background. The guy kept saying, "I love you, I love you, I love you."

"We get it. You love her. Now stop being so annoying," I said to the guy on TV.

Alexa started crying. She sobbed, "Oh, how sad! They're so in love and she's so sick."

"If this movie is so sad and it makes you cry, why do you watch it?" I asked.

"I love it," she sobbed.

"A nice cake would cheer you up. Would you like to buy cake mix to help my school and help yourself?" I asked.

"Do you have chocolate cake mix?" she asked.

I nodded.

"Is the cake easy to make?"

I nodded.

"Does your school need the money?"

I nodded again.

"That sounds great," Alexa said.

"So you'll buy some?" I asked.

"Nah. Now stop talking to me so I can cry in peace." She turned back to the TV.

The doorbell rang.

"How am I supposed to cry when I keep getting interrupted?" Alexa said. She went to the door and asked who was there.

A tiny, sweet voice said, "It's your neighbor, Sweet Molly May."

Alexa opened the door.

A cute, little kindergarten girl stood on our porch. "Would you like to buy some cake mix to support my school?" she asked.

"Sure. I'll buy a box," Alexa said. "Zeke, you should buy a box too."

"But I'm selling the same cake mix. And I'm your brother," I told Alexa.

She shrugged. "Sorry. You're just not as cute as Sweet Molly May."

Sweet Molly May smiled. She had dimples and was missing her front teeth. Smiling made her look even cuter. I bet everyone in the neighborhood would want to buy cake mix from her.

I told her, "Hey, Sweet Molly May. Don't go to any more houses. You'll get too tired. In fact, you should probably quit selling cake mix and go home."

"Okay," she said.

I sighed with relief. Getting Sweet Molly May to quit selling cake mix was easy.

"I'm already really tired. I've been to every house in the neighborhood," she said.

"Every house?" I asked.

She nodded again. "I want to win the tickets to Thrillsville."

"Aww, that's so cute. I'll buy two more boxes from you," Alexa said.

I banged my head against the wall.

Worrying Plus More WORRYING

Equals A LOT of Worrying

That is just WAY too much worrying!

The next day at school, Mr. McNutty said,
"It's finally time for our math lesson."

Owen Leach raised his hand. "I have a
math question. If I sold nine boxes of cake mix
yesterday, and each box cost five dollars, how
incredibly charming am I?"

"Not charming enough to interrupt my
math lesson," Mr. McNutty said. "But who can
tell me how much money Owen collected from
selling nine boxes at five dollars apiece?"

Grace Chang raised her hand. "He collected a small amount of money, compared to me. My mom and dad sold twenty boxes of cake mix."

"Yeah. Grace's mom and dad sold a lot of cake mix," Emma G. said.

"Yeah. They sold a lot of cake mix," Emma J. said.

"Never mind. Let's get started on math," Mr. McNutty said.

I raised my hand.

"Do you have a math question for me, Zeke?" the teacher asked.

"Yes. Well, it's not a math question

and it's not for you. But it's a question. Grace, did your mom and dad really walk around your neighborhood selling cake mix?" I asked.

"No. They sold it to the people they work with. And they're going to keep selling it. I will win those tickets to Thrillsville," Grace said.

"Yeah. Grace will win," Emma G. said.

"Yeah. Grace will win," Emma J. said.

"No. I will win those tickets," I said.

"How many boxes of cake mix have you sold?" Grace asked.

"A lot," I said. I'd sold only three boxes to my mom, but I planned to sell a lot more.

"Class. It's time for math. No more interruptions," Mr. McNutty said.

Grace's cell phone rang.

Mr. McNutty glared at her.

"I'll just be a minute," she told him. Then she said into the phone, "Hello, Mother."

Mr. McNutty crossed his arms.

Grace told her mother, "You sold only eight boxes of cake mix today? That's not enough. Work harder. Sell, sell, sell!" She clicked off the phone.

Mr. McNutty took it from her. "You can have your phone back after school."

"After school? I don't know if I can survive that long without my cell phone," she said.

"Most of us have survived our entire lives without one," I said.

Grace shuddered. "Horrors!"

Emma G. shuddered and said, "Yeah. Horrors!"

Emma J. shuddered and said, "Yeah. Horrors!"

"You don't even have cell phones," I said.

"Let's get back to our math problem," Mr. McNutty said. "If Owen sold nine boxes of cake mix, and each box cost five dollars, then —"

"Then Owen won't get tickets to Thrillsville," Grace said.

"Yeah. Owen won't get tickets," Emma G. said.

"Yeah. Owen won't get tickets," Emma J. said.

Victoria Crow raised her hand. She was the smartest kid in third grade. She said, "Nine multiplied by five equals forty-five. So Owen will have collected forty-five dollars."

Emma J. raised her hand. "He should really collect sales tax on that. At the rate of 6.25 percent, he should bring in forty-seven dollars and eighty-one cents."

Maybe Emma J. was really the smartest kid in third grade.

Aaron Glass raised his hand. "I sold two boxes of cake mix yesterday to my brother. He gave me a dollar for both. Is that a good deal?"

Aaron Glass was not the smartest kid in third grade. He wasn't even close. And he'd never win tickets to Thrillsville by selling only two boxes of cake mix.

I wouldn't win the tickets either, unless I started selling huge amounts of cake mix. I planned to go to every house in my neighborhood today.

But what if everyone already bought cake mix from Sweet Molly May? And even if I could sell cake mix to all my neighbors, that might not be enough. Owen could sell a lot of cake mix because he was incredibly charming. Grace was not incredibly charming, but her parents were selling a lot of cake mix for her.

"Zeke, are you paying attention?" Mr. McNutty asked.

"Yes," I said. I wasn't paying attention to the math lesson. But I *was* paying attention to the school fund-raiser contest. I'd have to work really hard to win the tickets to Thrillsville.

After school, Mom gave me a banana and cheese cubes for snack.

"I'd rather snack on cake," I said. "You should use the cake mixes you bought. And then you should buy many more cake mixes."

"Cake isn't healthy. It should be eaten only once in awhile, as a special treat," Mom said.

"That reminds me of a Princess Sing-Along song," my little sister, Mia, said.

Before I could stop her, she sang in a screechy voice: "You shouldn't eat too much sugar, la la la. Also, never eat your boogers, la la la."

I rolled my eyes. Then I said, "Can we walk around the neighborhood now, Mom? I need to sell a lot of cake mix."

"I'm ready to go. I'll sing Princess Sing-Along songs along the way," Mia said.

That sounded like total torture for me and my ears.

"Waggles can come too. I'll dress him up," Mia said.

That sounded like total torture for me and my eyes. I said, "Mia, you should stay here with Alexa. I'll be walking really fast around the entire neighborhood. You and Waggles won't be able to keep up with me."

Luckily for me and my ears and my eyes, Mom agreed with me. She made Mia and Waggles stay home.

I walked next door and knocked on the front door. A teenage boy opened it. "Hey, Zeke. Hello, Mrs. Meeks," he said.

I didn't know the boy's name. He and his brothers were triplets who looked exactly alike. The guy at the door was either Andrew, Austin, or Alex. I said, "Hi. I'm selling cake mix to help my school. It comes in vanilla, chocolate, and lemon flavors. Each box costs five dollars."

"My brothers and I love making cake. And that cake mix makes really good cake." He rubbed his stomach.

"You've used the cake mix before?" I asked.

"My brothers and I made cake last night. We bought ten boxes from Sweet Molly May. Don't you think she's adorable?"

"Yes, she's adorable," I said with a frown.

"We spent all our money yesterday," he said.

The Burkes lived in the next house. They had five children. I bet they ate a lot of cake.

Mrs. Burke answered the door. She was holding a baby. A little kid clung to her leg. "Hello," she said.

Mrs. Burke scowled. "How do you know what we eat? Young man, it's none of your business whether my family eats cake."

The baby started crying.

"And now you've made my baby cry," Mrs. Burke said. "I refuse to answer your nosy questions about my family's eating habits. It's time for you to go."

"But I —"

She slammed the door in my face.

That hadn't gone very well.

I really wanted to win the tickets to Thrillsville. So I went to every house in my neighborhood. Some people didn't answer their doors. A lot of my neighbors had already bought cake mix from Sweet Molly May. Other people said the cake mix cost too much money or was too unhealthy or too hard to make.

Guess how many boxes of cake mix I sold to my neighbors?

Did you guess yet?

I hope you didn't pick a high number.

It was a very low number. It was zero. Not a single one of my neighbors bought cake mix from me.

At least my mother bought another box, but that's only because she felt sorry for me.

We walked back home. I told my mom, "My life is so hard compared to everyone else's life. Sweet Molly May can sell things just by looking cute and little. Grace Chang doesn't even have to walk around her neighborhood. Her parents are selling cake mix for her."

"You have it easy compared with some people," Mom said.

"Think about your great-grandmother. She can't take care of herself very well anymore. She had to move out of the house she'd lived in for a long time."

"That does sound pretty bad," I said.

Mom nodded. "She's lonely in her nursing home. She would love to see you."

"Okay, I'll visit Great-Gran tomorrow," I said.

Mom smiled.

"Good. I'm proud of you," she said.

I didn't think Mom would be so proud of me if she knew the real reason I wanted to visit Great-Gran. I hoped to sell cake mix to her and everyone else in her nursing home.

NE MIST

Zebe's
CANE
Tricks

The next day, Mom drove me to Great-Gran's new nursing home. I was a little scared to go there. The last time I'd seen Great-Gran, she'd given me a big kiss on my cheek. She had forgotten to put in her false teeth.

Have you ever been kissed by someone with no teeth? If you haven't, you're lucky. Being kissed by a toothless person feels weird.

"If Great-Gran isn't wearing her false teeth, do I have to let her kiss me?" I asked my mom.

"Of course you do. I'm proud of you for visiting her today. It's the right thing to do," Mom said.

I thought it was the right thing to do in order to sell cake mix. I asked my mom, "How many people live in the nursing home?"

"About a hundred. And a lot of other people work there," she said.

I wanted to sell cake mix to every person there.

Mom parked the car, and we got out. The nursing home looked nice, like a hotel. It had a big, green lawn and bright, white tables and chairs in front.

"What do you have in your hand?" Mom asked me.

"An order form for cake mix. Great-Gran might want to buy a box or two," I said.

I hoped she'd want to buy more than that. Ten boxes would be good.

"Great-Gran can't do any baking in her nursing home. She has no use for cake mix," said Mom.

I frowned. I wondered if she'd buy my cake mix anyway.

An old man came up to us. "You were just here a few days ago. Are you back already?" he asked Mom.

Mom smiled. "It's a nice place to visit. This is my son, Zeke."

The man stuck out his hand.

I shook it. It felt dry and wrinkled.

"Nice to meet you, Zebe," he said. "I'm Mr. Cowan."

"Zeke," I said.

"What's up, Zebe?" he asked.

"I'm selling cake mix to help my school."

He cupped his hand over his ear. "Did you say you're selling cape tricks? Is that something magicians use in their acts?"

"Cake mix," I said.

"Cave mints? What are those? Mints for miners in caves?"

"Not cave mints. I'm selling cake mix," I said loudly.

"Cane mist sounds useful. A mist to spray on canes to keep them clean."

"I'm selling cake mix!" I shouted.

"You shouldn't shout. It's rude," Mr. Cowan said.

"Would you like to buy some cake mix?" I asked.

"I don't have a cane. I don't need cleaning mist for it. But other people here might like your cane mist," he said.

"Thanks anyway. Goodbye, Mr. Cowan," I said.

"Goodbye, Zebe." Mr. Cowan shook my hand again.

The trip to the nursing home was not starting out well.

We found Great-Gran sitting in a wheelchair in the social hall. "Zeke, it's great to see you. Come here and let me kiss you," she said.

I slowly walked over to her.

She kissed me on the cheek.

Phew. She had put in her false teeth.

Mom and I sat at a table with her.

"What's that in your hand?" Great-Gran asked me.

"It's an order form for cake mix. I'm selling it to help my school."

"How much does it cost?" she asked.

"Five dollars."

"I could get cake mix at the market for much less money. Why should I spend extra on your cake mix?" she asked.

"It makes delicious cake," I said.

"Have you tried it?"

"No," I admitted.

She shook her head. "You know as much about the cake you're trying to sell as I know about rap music. In other words, not much. Do you know if the cake is easy to make?" she asked.

"I'm sure it is," I said.

"Have you tried making it yourself?"

I shook my head.

"Does the cake come with frosting, or do I have to buy that separately?" she asked.

I shrugged.

"Your sales ability is like my ability to ride a unicycle. In other words, it's pretty poor. To be a good salesperson, you should know all about your product. And you should show it off to your customers. When I used to sell makeup, I tried it on myself first, and I gave out samples to my customers."

"You used to sell makeup?" I asked.

"I did, for many years. I sold so much makeup that the company I worked for gave me a fancy car as a bonus."

"So should I bake a cake from one of the mixes and give out sample slices?" I asked.

"Exactly," Great-Gran said.

"Do you have any other advice for me?"

"Work really hard. Walk around your entire neighborhood."

I sighed. "A tiny, little girl did that the day before I did. She was so adorable that the neighbors bought cake mix from her instead of me."

"That's a problem. You're cute, but you're just not as adorable as a tiny, little girl," Great-Gran said.

I sighed again. "Maybe I should give up."

"Don't give up. You have a tiny, little sister who's adorable," Great-Gran said.

"My sister isn't adorable. She's annoying."

"She's annoying to you, because you're her brother. But I bet other people find her adorable. You have a dog too, right?" Great-Gran asked.

I nodded.

"Go out and sell your cake mix. Bring your little sister and dog along with you. Make sure they look as adorable as possible," she said.

"Thanks for the advice," I said.

"You're welcome. And I'll buy a box of cake mix if I can come over to your house to bake it."

"That would be great," I said.

Great-Gran's fingers didn't work very well, so I filled out the order form for her.

Then Great-Gran said, "I bet you'd make a good cribbage partner. Let's play a game against your mom."

"I can't. I don't know how."

"Never say you can't do something. A good salesperson always tries. After I teach you cribbage, I bet you'll be great at it."

"Maybe I can teach you about rap music," I told Great-Gran.

She smiled and said, "I would like that. But I hope you don't suggest I try riding a unicycle too."

I smiled back at her. "Maybe next year."

Gran taught me how to play cribbage. I learned the game pretty fast.

After a few games, Mom said, "We need to go."

"But we've only been here a few minutes," I said.

"It's actually been two hours," Mom said.

Great-Gran patted my hand. "Time flies when you're having fun."

On the way out, we ran into Mr. Cowan again. He said, "I hope you had a nice visit, Zebe. I bet you'll sell a lot of that cane mist."

"I had a great visit. And once I use my Great-Gran's ideas, I think I'll sell a lot more," I said.

Great-Gran's
Gran's
GREAT IDEAS

I followed Great-Gran's suggestions. With Mom's help, I made a cake from one of the mixes she'd bought. I found out that the cake mix came with frosting mix. I made the frosting too. It was pretty easy. Then I tasted the cake. It was delicious.

Mia asked, "Can I try the cake too?"

"Only if you come with me when I sell cake mix," I said.

"A few days ago, you told me I had to stay home because I was too young," Mia said.

"That was a few days ago. You're older now," I said.

"I'll try to act really old," she said.

I shook my head. "No. You should act really young, like an adorable, tiny, little girl. You should bring one of your dolls with you."

She clapped her hands. "Yay! I know just who I'm bringing."

Then she got out her Princess Sing-Along doll and pushed the button on its stomach. It started screeching a song. Mia screeched along with her doll. "Even on a winter day, la la la, you should go outside and play, la la la. But wear thick snow boots and warm clothes, la la la, so frostbite won't destroy your toes, la la la."

Princess Sing-Along songs were so annoying. Taking Mia with me today was going to be awful. But Great-Gran had told me to do it. She'd sold so much makeup, she'd won a car. If she could do that, I could win tickets to Thrillsville.

Then I told Mia something that I never, ever, ever thought I'd say: "We're taking our dog along. Would you please dress him in something really cute?"

Mia's eyebrows scrunched together. "I thought you didn't like when I dress him up."

"Usually I don't like it. But today I do."

Mia clapped again. "This is the best day ever."

For *her* it was the best day ever. For *me* it might be the worst day ever.

Mom drove us to a neighborhood far from ours. Hopefully, no one had tried to sell cake mix there yet.

I sat in the backseat, holding a box filled with small slices of cake, plastic forks, and napkins. Next to me, Mia sat in her carseat. She wore a blue and white dress that made her look like a tiny, little sailor. I had to admit it was adorable. Waggles stood in the front seat with his face out the window.

He wore a big, lacy bow on his head. I thought he looked ridiculous. But Mom and Mia said he was adorable.

Mom parked the car and watched as I went to the first house and knocked on the door. Behind me stood Mia, holding her Princess Sing-Along doll in one hand and Waggles's leash in the other hand.

I hoped Great-Gran knew what she was talking about. I didn't know what I would do, if this didn't work.

"Hello," I said to the woman who opened the door. "I'm Zeke Meeks. This is my tiny, little, adorable sister, Mia, and my darling, dressed-up dog, Waggles. We're selling delicious cake mix to help my school."

"Another school fund-raiser." The lady shook her head.

"This cake is easy to make and really yummy. Please try some. I baked it myself." I handed the woman a slice of cake, a fork, and a napkin.

After eating the cake, she said, "This *is* tasty. How much does it cost?"

"It comes with frosting mix, so it's really a bargain. It's only five dollars."

"I don't know if I want to buy that," the woman said.

"Please buy cake mix to help the sweet, little, needy schoolchildren," Mia pleaded.

Waggles let out a cute yap.

The woman smiled. "How can I say no to such adorable children and that darling dog? Okay, I'll buy a box of cake mix."

"How about one of each flavor?" I asked.

"All right. You're a good salesperson."

I smiled as I handed her the order form. "Thanks. I get my sales talent from my great-grandmother," I said.

We walked to the next house. I sold cake mix there too. I sold it at the next house and the next and the next. At the sixth house, the woman asked Mia, "What's your doll's name?"

"Princess Sing-Along. She sings great songs. So do I," Mia said.

The woman patted Mia's head. "I'll buy your cake mix if you sing a song for me."

Mia sang: "Some words are so ugly and naughty, la la la. They make your mouth seem like a potty, la la la. So you should try hard to act smart, la la la, and not say words like *poop* or *fart*, la la la."

Mia took a bow. Then she asked, "Will you buy two boxes of cake mix if I sing another song?"

The woman shook her head. "I'll buy two boxes of cake mix if you *don't* sing another song."

"Thanks. That's a deal," I said.

We walked to a lot more houses. Every so often, Mia said she was too tired to walk anymore. I told her what Great-Gran had told me: "Never say you can't do something. A good salesperson always tries."

After a few hours of hard work, my order form was completely filled up. It had been a very successful day.

"You must be tired," Mom said as we walked back to the car.

I shrugged. "Not really."

On the way home, I closed my eyes and imagined myself winning the Thrillsville tickets. I pictured myself walking into Thrillsville. I imagined getting in line for the new ride there.

Then I fell asleep.

Zeke Meeks
vs.
Grace Chang's
Mom and Dad

If you think Grace Chang is scary . . .

↓

Her parents sound terrifying. I imagine hooks
for hands and vampire fangs to suck people's
blood. Terrifying . . .

After selling so much cake mix, I was in a great mood at school the next day.

Then I saw Grace Chang. She said, "My parents sold a lot more cake mix to people they work with. In exchange, they had to buy a bunch of stuff for other fund-raisers. We now have a box of greeting cards to help a middle school, cookie dough to help high school cheerleaders, popcorn for the Boy Scouts, a cookbook, candles, a tote bag, and carrot seeds. But it was worth it. I'm going to win the tickets to Thrillsville."

That made me nervous. I asked Grace, "How many boxes did your parents sell?"

"None of your business. But it's more than you could ever sell," she said.

"Yeah, Zeke. It's none of your business," Emma G. said.

"Yeah, Zeke. It's more than you could ever sell," Emma J. said.

I frowned. What if Grace's parents had sold more cake mix than I'd sold yesterday? I was too tired to sell any more boxes before the contest ended tomorrow.

Then I thought about Great-Gran. She didn't give up. If she had been too tired to sell more makeup, she never would have won a car. I still had one more day to outsell Grace's parents. I decided to make another cake and sell more cake mix after school.

Mom wasn't very happy when she heard my plan. "But I want to see your great-grandmother today," she said.

"That's perfect," I said. "Great-Gran wants to make cake at our house. We can invite her over today. And she can help me sell cake mix."

"I bet she'll love that," Mom said.

"Me too," I said.

So we picked up Great-Gran from the nursing home, brought her to our house, and made cake together.

As we waited for it to bake in the oven, Great-Gran gave me more advice. She said, "When you talk to people, keep in mind how good the cake smells while it's baking and how delicious it tastes. You need to believe in what you're selling."

Then she told me I also had to believe in myself. She had me look at myself in the bathroom mirror and repeat, "I'm a great salesperson," over and over. Soon I really believed it.

"Now that I've taught you about selling things, you need to keep your promise to me," she said.

"What promise?" I asked.

"You said you'd teach me about rap music."

"Rappers act real tough and move with a swagger. They talk about their homies. That means their friends and families. And they say 'yo' a lot," I told Great-Gran.

My sister Alexa played some rap music. Great-Gran and I sang along.

NOW TRY TO MAKE UP YOUR OWN RAP SONG.

Great-Gran thought about it awhile. Then she used a spatula as a pretend microphone and rapped a song: "I may move kind of slow. But I got swagger, yo. Homie Zeke is a sales pro. I taught him all that I know. He takes in a lot of dough. Selling cake mix, yo, yo, yo."

Great-Gran wasn't exactly ready to be a rap star, but she wasn't bad.

Once the cake was baked, frosted, and sliced, I went out to sell the cake mix. Mom, Mia, Waggles, and Great-Gran came with me.

"I'm glad you're here. Your sales tips will help me," I told Great-Gran.

"Word, homie," she said. She was getting carried away with the rap stuff. "Also, people will feel sorry for me in my wheelchair. That will help sell more cake mix," she added. She put on a bonnet to look extra sweet.

We went to a lot of houses. Great-Gran told people in her sweetest voice, "I hope you'll help my darling, little great-grandson and his wonderful school."

Usually they did.

We all got really tired. Even Waggles started to walk slowly. But Great-Gran kept convincing us to keep going. We didn't stop until it got dark outside and Mom said we had to go home.

By that time, I'd sold even more cake mix than I had yesterday. I thought I had a good chance of winning the Thrillsville tickets — unless Sweet Molly May or Grace Chang's parents or someone I didn't even know about outsold me.

I just had to wait until tomorrow to find out.

FOUR Tickets
for SIX People
Equals a VERY
Hard Math
Problem

No matter how you work the
numbers, it doesn't add up.

In class the next day, it was almost impossible to pay attention. Even after we turned in our order forms, I kept wondering if I'd sold enough cake mix to win the contest. I'd have to wait until the end of the day. That's when the principal was supposed to announce who sold the most cake mix. I didn't know if I could survive that long. I thought I could be the first kid ever to actually die of curiosity.

At recess, Grace Chang said, "Don't worry, Zeke. I didn't sell much cake mix."

That was a surprise. "You didn't?" I asked.

"*I* didn't. But *my parents* sold a ton of it. I'm sure they sold more than anyone else. Bah ha ha ha." She had an evil laugh. It gave me the chills.

After I finished shivering, I said, "I sold a lot of cake mix too."

Grace shook her head. "But less than my parents sold. Don't worry. I'll tell you all about the new ride at Thrillsville. It will be almost as good as going there yourself. *Almost.* Bah ha ha."

I shivered again. Listening to Grace Chang was a waste of good recess time. I went to the basketball court to shoot hoops with Hector.

"Hi, Zeke. Do you think you'll win the contest?" Hector asked as he dribbled the basketball.

The ball was very flat. I stole it from him easily. I said, "I sold a lot of cake mix. I might win."

"The winner gets four tickets to Thrillsville. Who will you invite?" he asked.

"You, of course. You're my best friend. And Charlie, my second best friend. A grown-up has to come along. So I'd have to invite my mom too."

"I really, really hope you win," Hector said. Then he stole the basketball from me.

I don't remember much about the rest of the day. Mr. McNutty might have taught math, read a book to us, and talked about science and history. Or he might not have. I wasn't paying attention. All I could think about was the fundraising contest.

Finally, the principal's voice came over the loudspeaker. She thanked everyone for selling cake mix and said we'd raised a lot of money. Then she said, "Four tickets to Thrillsville go to the student who sold the most boxes of cake mix. That student is . . ." She paused.

Grace stood up and smiled. Then she took a long bow.

"Zeke Meeks," the principal said.

I rushed out of my seat and jumped up and down.

Grace's mouth dropped open. She glared at me. Then she thrust her hand toward me. Her long, sharp, evil fingernails were pointed right at my face.

But I was in much too good of a mood to worry about that.

"Thrillsville, here I come!" I shouted.

I couldn't wait to tell Great-Gran. Her advice and our hard work had paid off.

After school, I picked up the Thrillsville tickets from the school office. Then Charlie and I got in my mom's minivan. Since we lived across the street from each other, Charlie and I carpooled a lot.

I waved the Thrillsville tickets in front of my mom's face and shouted, "I won the contest!"

"Terrific!" Mom said.

"Yay! I get to go to Thrillsville!" Mia shouted from the back of the minivan.

"Actually, I promised to take Hector and Charlie to Thrillsville. They're my two best friends. I can't change my mind now," I said.

"Yes, you can," Mia said. "Yesterday you told me to never say you can't do something. I walked all over two big neighborhoods with you. I wore my cutest clothes and brought my doll and dressed up Waggles to help you out."

She had a point. But taking my friends to Thrillsville would be a lot more fun than taking Mia. I told her, "You're not even big enough for the scary rides."

"I'm big enough for other rides. And you said I was big enough to do all that walking the last two days."

"Zeke, if your little sister helped you win the contest, you should give her a ticket," Charlie said.

"Don't you want to go to Thrillsville?" I asked.

"I don't want to go instead of Mia. She deserves a ticket to Thrillsville."

Mom looked at me. "Do you know who else deserves to go?"

I frowned. "Instead of Hector?"

Mom nodded.

I did know who else deserved to go — an old lady who taught me a lot about sales. I sighed. It wouldn't be much fun to go to Thrillsville with my mom, my little sister, and my great-grandmother. But it was the right thing to do.

"If Hector's a good friend, he'll understand why you won't give him a ticket," Mom said.

"Yeah. I'm a good friend and I understand why you won't give me a ticket," Charlie said.

I smiled at her. "How can I make things up to you?"

"Why don't you bake me a cake? I hear you're pretty good at it."

"Okay. I'll bake one for Hector also," I said. "I have to share my tickets with Mia and my great-grandmother."

"Maybe I'll win the next contest. I'm sure there will be another school fund-raiser soon," Charlie said.

Mom sighed. "I'm sure there will be many, many more fund-raisers."

A KILLER Day

9

On Saturday morning, Mom, Mia, and I picked up Great-Gran at her nursing home. We put her wheelchair into our trunk and started on the long drive to Thrillsville.

"Are you sure you don't want to wait a few weeks to go to Thrillsville? It will be very crowded there today because the new ride is opening. I heard that the line for Mount Killer could be three hours long," Mom said.

"I'm sure I want to go today," I said. I had already told everyone in my class that I'd be on the Mount Killer ride on opening day.

Mia screeched a Princess Sing-Along song: "Take a bath every night, la la la. So you won't smell like a fright, la la la."

"Mia, don't sing dumb Princess Sing-Along songs," I said.

"Princess Sing-Along songs aren't dumb," Mia said.

"Yes, they are," I said.

"No, they're not. *You're* dumb," she said.

"*You're* dumb," I said.

"*You're* —"

Great-Gran let out a loud whistle. Then she said, "Arguing is dumb. I have an idea. I've learned Princess Sing-Along songs from Mia and rap songs from Zeke. Now I'll teach you kids an old song called 'Minnie the Moocher.'" And she did.

To tell you the truth, the song was pretty dumb. Most of the words were things like, "Hydie, hydie, ho," and, "Oh, oh, oh," and, "Yeah, yeah." It was so dumb that soon we were all laughing.

"I could make up a better song than that," I said. I started singing about Minnie the Moocher's pet, Morris the Mule. I added, "Ooh, ooh, ooh," and, "Shoobie woobie."

Then Mom made up a song about Minnie's other pet, Myrna the Monkey. She sang, "Wah, wah, wah."

When we saw the big crowds at the park, Mom said, "The Mount Killer ride is going to have a killer line." She was right. The line was huge. A sign at the end of the line said Current Wait: 3 hours.

"We don't have to stand in that long line," Great-Gran said.

"Princess Sing-Along says to wait your turn," Mia said. Then she sang, "People who cut in line, la la la, behave like nasty swine, la la la."

"We won't cut in line. We'll use a different entrance for people in wheelchairs," Great-Gran said.

She led me to a separate entrance. Mom waited outside with Mia, who was too little for the ride.

After only a few minutes, Great-Gran and I
went on Mount Killer. It was very scary. It had
dark tunnels, crazy twists, and sharp drops. It
made me scream and feel sick to my stomach.

I thought it was the best ride ever.

"Whoa! That was more fun than a barrel of monkeys in a room full of clowns. Thanks for inviting me along," Great-Gran said.

"Thanks for helping me win the tickets. This is the best day at Thrillsville ever," I said.

Don't tell Hector or Charlie, but I was glad I'd taken Great-Gran to Thrillsville instead of them.

My Hero,
the
Interrupting
PRINCIPAL

Shocker, I know. Believe me, I'm shocked too.

At recess on Monday, my friends and I tried to find a good basketball. The first basketball was completely flat. Two others were mostly flat.

Owen pointed across the playground and said, "That's the only good basketball."

Hector, Charlie, and I nodded. Grace Chang had taken the ball at the beginning of recess. She held it while she talked to Emma G. and Emma J. Every so often, she laughed her evil "Bah ha ha ha" laugh.

"Grace isn't even playing basketball. You should ask her for the ball," I told Owen.

"Why don't *you* ask her for the ball?" he said.

I shrugged. But we both knew why not. Grace Chang was evil. So were her long, sharp fingernails. Someone who asked her for the ball could be someone with his face ripped off. I did not want to be that someone.

I tried to bounce one of the mostly flat basketballs. It mostly lay on the ground. "I was bouncing harder in my seat on the Mount Killer ride on Saturday," I said.

"You're so lucky," Owen said.

"And he got to go on the ride three times," Charlie added.

"Without waiting in the long line," Hector said.

"How did you sell so much cake mix?" Owen asked.

"A wise woman gave me her ancient secrets," I said.

"His great-grandmother used to sell stuff. She gave him advice," Hector explained.

The bell rang, so we had to return to class.

Once again, Mr. McNutty said the three worst words in the universe: "Time for math."

I slowly got out my math book. I wished we could have another fire drill or assembly. I wouldn't have minded if someone threw up on a desk again — as long as it wasn't *my* desk. I wished we could have anything right now besides a math lesson.

Then the principal's voice came on over the loudspeaker. She said, "I have an important announcement."

"Yahoo!" I yelled.

"You haven't even heard what the announcement is," Mr. McNutty said.

"It doesn't matter. As long as it interrupts math, I'll be happy," I said.

"What if the principal announces that from now on, we'll have school six days a week?"

"I wouldn't be happy about that," I admitted.

The principal said, "The PTA used the money from the cake mix sales to buy math flashcards, math computer programs, graph paper, rulers, and other math supplies. Thanks to your fund-raising efforts, every class will spend more time on math."

I groaned.

"We had a little money left over," the principal said. "So the PTA bought two new soccer balls, three big rubber balls, and five new basketballs. Have a nice day."

Everyone cheered.

"Time for math," Mr. McNutty said again.

I groaned again.

Then our classroom door opened. Mrs. Smedley, the PTA president, walked in. She said, "Your class raised more money than any other class. Zeke Meeks and Grace Chang should be especially proud for selling so much cake mix."

"Actually, I didn't sell any. My parents sold a lot though," Grace said.

"Well, thanks to Grace's parents and Zeke, your class gets a party," Mrs. Smedley said.

"But I'm trying to teach math now," Mr. McNutty said.

"That can wait. I made cake. Everyone gets a slice," Mrs. Smedley said.

I was really happy to skip a math lesson again. But I was also really tired of cake. I decided to save my slice for later. Hopefully, I could visit Great-Gran and give her the slice after school today.

ABOUT THE AUTHOR

D. L. Green lives in California with her husband, three children, silly dog, and a big collection of rubber chickens. She loves to read, write, and joke around.

ABOUT THE ILLUSTRATOR

Josh Alves LOVES roller coasters and would enjoy winning tickets to Thrillsville Amusement Park. He gets to draw in his studio in Maine where he lives with his incredible wife and their three amazing children.

WHAT IS THE WORST THING YOU'VE EVER HAD TO SELL?

(And other really important questions)

Write answers to these questions, or discuss them with your friends and classmates.

1. Schools are always asking kids to sell things. What's the worst thing you've ever had to sell?

2. What is the best fund-raiser you have ever heard of? A kiss-a-pig contest for teachers? A yummy bake sale? Something even better?

3. Who would you take to Thrillsville if you won tickets there?

4. Have you ever won a contest? What was the contest and what did you win?

BIG WORDS
according to Zeke

TRY USING THEM IN SENTENCES JUST LIKE I DO

<u>ABILITY</u>: A special skill you have that helps you do something. Mia has the ability to annoy me every day.

<u>ADORABLE</u>: A word that girls use to describe things that they think are super cute. But adorable things are actually usually annoying and somewhat gross.

<u>ANCIENT</u>: Super-duper old, like Great-Gran.

<u>ANNOYING</u>: Things that are annoying bug you so much you think you might lose it!

<u>ASSEMBLY</u>: A special meeting at school. Sometimes they are exciting, but sometimes they are lame.

<u>ASSIGNMENT</u>: Homework your teacher asks you to do. Victoria Crow probably cries on nights there are no assignments.

<u>AUDITORIUM</u>: A large room in our school where we have assemblies, watch plays, and other stuff for the whole school.

<u>CONVINCING</u>: Getting someone to do something that he doesn't want to. Sometimes begging is involved.

<u>CRIBBAGE</u>: A card game that old people like.

<u>CURIOSITY</u>: A really bad need to find something out. I think you might die from extreme curiosity.

The school loudspeaker can also sound like it's screeching.

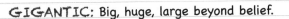

FUND-RAISING: Raising money to help out your school or club or something like that. My mom says we have WAY too much fund-raising at our school.

GIGANTIC: Big, huge, large beyond belief.

HORRORS: Things that are very scary, like insects.

INCREDIBLY: Super-duper, very much.

INSULT: To say or do something that made a person feel bad. Note: I said a PERSON, not Princess Sing-Along!

INTERRUPTED: Started talking when someone else was talking. Grown-ups tend to not like when you interrupt, but I don't see what the big deal is.

RELIEF: The feeling you get when something you are worried about goes away.

SCOWLED: Frowned with your whole face.

SCREECHING: Loud and high-pitched and awful! In other words, everything that has to do with Princess Sing-Along.

SHUDDERED: Shook out of fear, like when Grace Chang waves her fingernails at me.

SURVIVE: Live despite an incredible hardship, like not having a phone for a day.

SWAGGER: A really cool way of walking, sitting, and doing everything.

SWINE: Just another word for "pig."

Elephant Toothpaste!

Grandparents really don't like it if you sit around all day watching TV or playing video games when you visit them. So it's best to have some fun activities planned. The cool thing about grandparents, though, is they will totally let you make a mess — which makes this the perfect project to do with good old Gran!

What you need:

- an empty soda bottle, washed

- a cake pan

- a glass jar or similar container

- funnel

- 2 tablespoons warm water

- 1 teaspoon yeast

- 1/2 cup 6% hydrogen peroxide (note: you must use 6% or more)

- Food coloring

- squirt of dish soap

What you do:

1. Set the bottle in the middle of the pan.

2. In the glass jar, combine water and yeast. Swirl them together for a minute.

3. Mix the hydrogen peroxide, 4-5 drops food coloring, and dish soap in the soda bottle.

4. Pour the yeast mixture into the soda bottle. And get ready to be amazed! The mixture will create a big, foaming mix. It looks like toothpaste for elephants!

If your grandparent still isn't convinced this is a good idea, just tell him or her it is a science experiment in reactions. Who can resist a learning opportunity?

AWESOME HAIR

CHARMING SMILE

Zeke Meeks

COOLEST THI
GRADER YOU'
EVER MEET